THE ADVENTURES OF
DUKE,
THE THERAPY DOG:

DUKE FINDS A HOME

By Allison McGill

Illustrated by John Paul Snead

ISBN: 978-1-4834-9754-9 (sc)
ISBN: 978-1-4834-9753-2 (hc)
ISBN: 978-1-4834-9755-6 (e)

Library of Congress Control Number: 2019901306

Lulu Publishing Services rev. date: 02/12/2019

THE ADVENTURES OF DUKE, THE THERAPY DOG:

DUKE FINDS A HOME

For Jack, who
misses his puppy

My name is Duke.

Before I found my forever home, I was a nameless puppy who wasn't treated very well.

I would lie down in the dirt, hungry and thirsty, wondering if I would ever find a home with a family that would take care of me and that I could take care of.

One day, people from a wonderful rescue group saved me!

They gave me food and water,
which tasted extra good because
I was so hungry and thirsty!

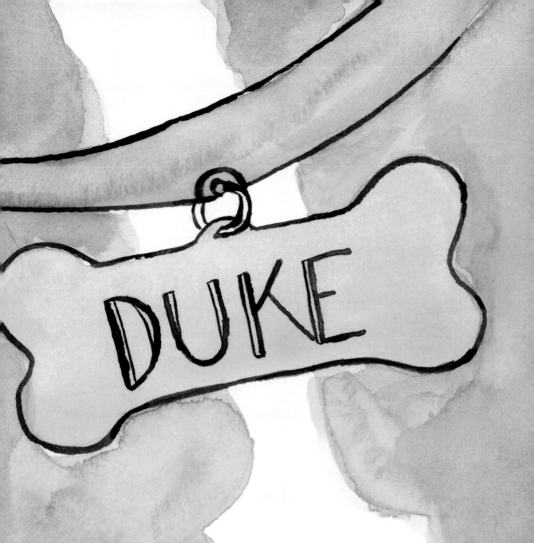

My foster parents nursed me
back to health and named me
Duke. I was ready to be adopted!

A couple, Joe and Alli, wanted
to adopt a rescued dog.

And they wanted to meet me!

Alli paced back and forth,

back and forth,

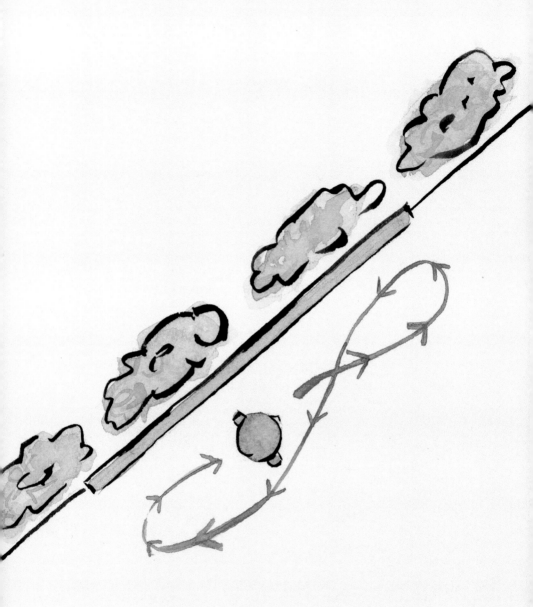

and back and forth some more

as she waited for me and my foster
parents to come to their home.
She was excited to meet me!

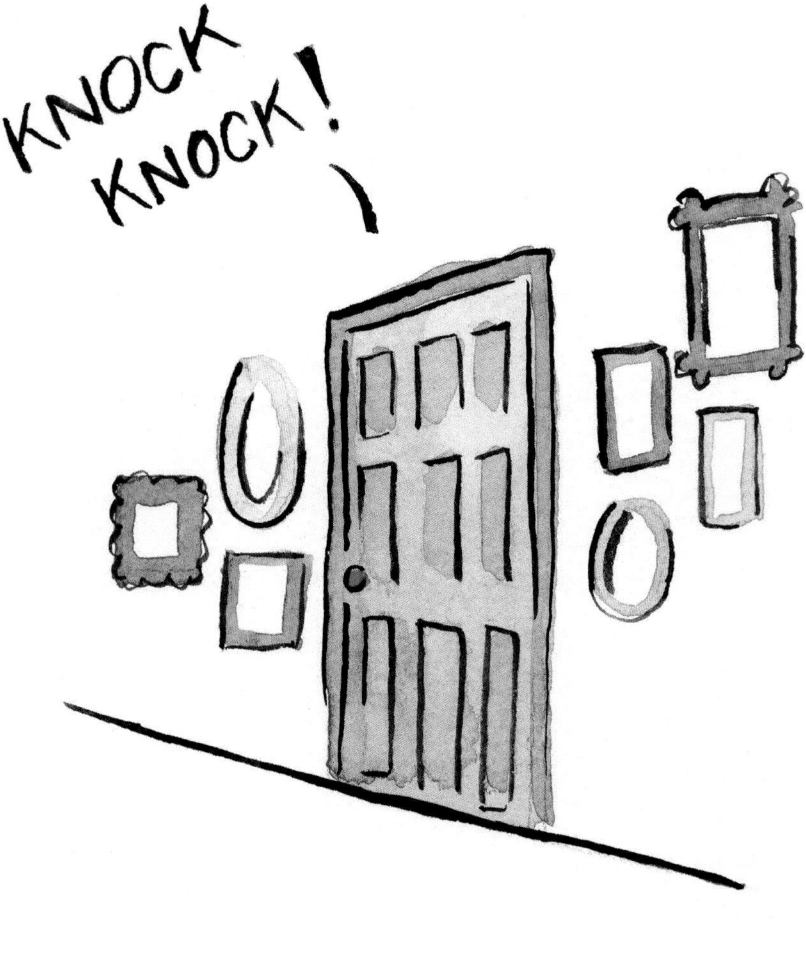
KNOCK
KNOCK!

Within seconds, everyone knew
I had found my forever home!

I went from
not being
treated well to

sleeping in the bed with them

and snuggling on the couch with them while they watch television.

When I am really relaxed and
feeling safe and secure,

I fall asleep
with my tongue
hanging out of
my mouth!

My new family
takes me for
long walks.

They make sure I always have enough food and water,

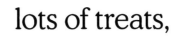

lots of treats,

and toys to play
with or snuggle!

I even have gifts and a stocking
on Christmas morning!

I love my forever family,
and they love me.

I can't believe how much my life has changed thanks to the rescue, my foster parents, and my forever home.

I am glad I was rescued
and adopted!

I now have a home with
people to take care of me,

and I can take care of them.

Exactly what I had hoped for!

To be continued…

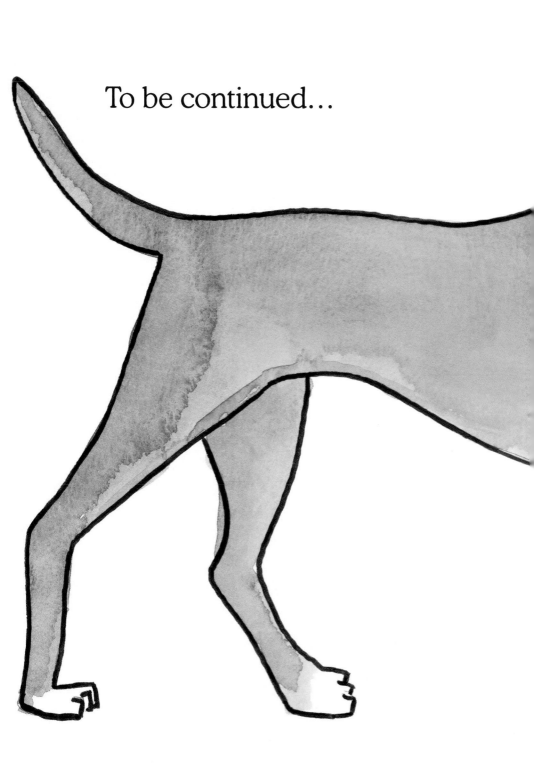

The Atlanta Boxer Rescue was founded in 2008. The first year, they rescued forty dogs. Now, they rescue more than 150 dogs a year. In 2011, they rescued our Duke. We are proud to partner with them by donating 20 percent of the profits of this book to them. For more information, visit atlantaboxerrescue.org.

Author Allison McGill likes books, macaroni and cheese, roller coasters, cookies, the movie "Elf," jokes, and dogs.

Illustrator John Paul Snead, some people call him JP, likes hanging out with his friends, stepping on crunchy fall leaves, and eating brussels sprouts!